Bill's Bike

by Andy Blackford

Illustrated by Hannah Wood

FRANKLIN WATTS
LONDON • SYDNEY

Notes on the series

TIDDLERS are structured to provide support for children who are starting to read on their own. The stories may also be used for sharing with children.

Starting to read alone can be daunting. **TIDDLERS** help by listing the words in the book for a check before reading, and by providing visual support and repeating words and phrases. These books will both develop confidence and encourage reading and rereading for pleasure.

If you are reading this book with a child, here are a few suggestions:

1. Make reading fun! Choose a time to read when you and the child are relaxed and have time to share the story.
2. Talk about the story before you start reading. Look at the cover and the blurb. What might the story be about? Why might the child like it?
3. Look also at the list of words below - can the child tackle most of the words?
4. Encourage the child to retell the story, using the jumbled picture puzzle.
5. Give praise! Remember that small mistakes need not always be corrected.

Here is a list of the words in this story.

Common words:

and	help	one
Dad	I	said
had	it	to
he	now	

Other words:

bike	happy	three
Bill	need	two
birthday	only	wheels
four	rode	works

3

Bill's bike had four wheels.

4

Bill rode.

"I only need three wheels!" he said.

Bill rode and rode.

11

"I only need two wheels!" he said.

Bill rode and rode
and rode.

"I only need one wheel!" he said.

16

17

"Help!" said Bill.

19

"It works now!" said Dad.

Puzzle Time

Can you find these
pictures in the story?

Which pages are the
pictures from?

Turn over for answers!

The pictures come from these pages:

a. pages 12 and 13

b. pages 18 and 19

c. pages 16 and 17

d. pages 6 and 7

First published in 2010 by
Franklin Watts
338 Euston Road
London
NW1 3BH

Franklin Watts Australia
Level 17/207 Kent Street
Sydney
NSW 2000

Text © Andy Blackford 2010
Illustration © Hannah Wood 2010

A CIP catalogue record for this book is
available from the British Library.

ISBN 978 0 7496 9386 2 (hbk)
ISBN 978 0 7496 9398 5 (pbk)

Series Editor: Jackie Hamley
Series Advisor: Catherine Glavina
Series Designer: Peter Scoulding

Printed in China

Franklin Watts is a division of Hachette Children's Books,
an Hachette UK company. www.hachette.co.uk